G7932l

For Iris
N.G.

For Vivien
M.R.

Macmillan Publishing Company
866 Third Avenue, New York, NY 10022
First published in 1990 by Walker Books Ltd.
London, England
Printed and bound in Hong Kong
First American Edition

10   9   8   7   6   5   4   3   2   1

Library of Congress Cataloging-in-Publication Data
Gray, Nigel.
Little Pig's tale / written by Nigel Gray;
illustrated by Mary Rees. — 1st American ed.
p.   cm.
Summary: Almost all Little Pig's attempts at finding
the right present for his mother's birthday fail,
but his last idea is just right.
ISBN 0-02-736942-0
[1. Pigs — Fiction.   2. Mothers and sons — Fiction.
3. Birthdays — Fiction.]
I. Rees, Mary, ill.   II. Title.
PZ7.G7813Li   1990   [E] — dc20
90-30642   CIP   AC

Little Pig's Tale

Written by
Nigel Gray

Illustrated by
Mary Rees

MACMILLAN PUBLISHING COMPANY
New York

On Monday, Little Pig's father told him,
"Next Sunday, it's your mother's birthday."

"Will she have a party?" asked Little Pig.

"No. I don't think she'll have a party,"
said Dad.

"Will she have a birthday cake with lots of
candles?"

"No. I don't think she'll want a cake with
lots of candles."

"Will we sing 'Happy Birthday to You'?"

"Yes. We must sing 'Happy Birthday to You.'"

"And will we give her presents?"

"Of course," said Dad. "I'll give her a
present. And you should give her a present, too."

"What will I give her?" asked Little Pig.
"I don't know," said Dad. "You'll have to
think of something."

On Tuesday, Little Pig tried to think of
something exciting. Perhaps his mother
would like an airplane so she could fly high,
high above the town . . .

or a rocket so she could explore the moon . . .

or a spaceship so she could venture
into outer space . . .

But Little Pig knew he couldn't really give her a spaceship, or a rocket, or even an airplane. For one thing, their garage was too small.

He'd have to think of something else.

On Wednesday, Little Pig thought of flowers and fruit. He'd give his mother an orchard—an orchard with pears and plums, apples and apricots, with daffodils and crocuses growing in the lush grass under the trees. He knew she'd like that because she was always weeding her window box, and growing plants in pots from apple seeds and cherry pits.

Little Pig went to see Mr. Green, the gardener.

"I'm sure your mother would love an orchard," said Mr. Green, "but your backyard is too small, and trees take years to grow. It was a good idea, Little Pig, but I'm afraid you'll have to think of something else."

On Thursday, Little Pig knew what he
had to do. He raided his piggy bank and
took his pennies to the store.
He would buy his mother a silk gown,
and a warm coat, and shiny shoes, and furry
gloves, and glittering jewels for her to wear
around her neck.

But Mr. Brown counted Little Pig's pennies and said, "I'm sorry, Little Pig, but you don't have enough money for any of those things."

"Not even for the gloves?" asked Little Pig.

"Not even for one glove," said Mr. Brown.

On Friday, Little Pig felt sad. In two days it would be his mother's birthday and Little Pig had nothing to give her. What was he to do? He asked his father.

"Why don't you make her something?" suggested Dad.

So Little Pig set to work.

He'd make her a useful box for keeping things in.

He fetched the tools, and found some old pieces of wood in the shed.

The wood splintered. The box broke.

He'd make her a beautiful necklace of beads.

He got the beads from an old jar and threaded them on a piece of string.

The string snapped, and the beads spilled all over the floor.

He'd do a painting in rainbow colors.

He got out his paints and a large sheet of white paper.

But he knocked over the pot of black paint and ruined his painting with an ugly splotch.

He'd bake some cupcakes.

He mixed up flour and milk and eggs and
raisins and dates, and greased the baking
pan with margarine.

But the cakes burned and came out of the
oven as hard as stones.

On Saturday, Little Pig was in despair.
He thought and thought until his brain hurt.
And then he had a wonderful idea.

On Sunday, it was Little Pig's mother's birthday. After breakfast Little Pig and Dad sang "Happy Birthday to You." Then Dad gave Mom a present . . . and while no one was looking, Little Pig slipped away.

He gathered together the things
he would need.

A piece of paper,

a pen,

and a red ribbon.

Mom unwrapped her gift. Inside was a watch.

"That's because I want you to have a good time," Dad said. And Mom gave Dad a kiss.

Then, on the table, Mom found a note. It said:

To Mother.
Your present is upstairs
in the bed.
Happy Birthday!
Lots of love from Little Pig.

Mom went up to the bedroom.

There was certainly something in the bed.

She pulled back the covers and there was...

Little Pig, with a red ribbon tied around
him in a bow. "Happy Birthday, Mom!"
said Little Pig.

"Oh, Little Pig," said Mom, "this is the
best present you could possibly have given me.
There's nothing in the world I'd rather have."

Mom hugged Little Pig and gave him a
big sloppy kiss.
And Little Pig beamed from ear to ear.